"It is easy to write about sex, much harder to write poetically about sexuality. The poems and the collection of line drawings in Marilyn Wolf's, *The Guy*, succeed in the latter with their exploration of a tension that surely lives at the heart of our species: loyalty vs lust."
— John Barr, author of *The Boxer of Quirinal*

"In this riveting book-length poem, Marilyn Wolf takes us on the emotional rollercoaster ride of a woman who comes out of a 'maelstrom of horror,' to rebuild her life in a new town with a new love – The Guy. But although the sex is great, he has a secret that threatens to hurl her back into a whirlpool of woe. Wolf's writing is reminiscent of Henry Miller."
— David Allen, author of *Deadlines Amuse Me*

"A tantalizing tale of the cycle of loss and recovery. Slip into something comfortable and devour."
— Mike Nierste, author of *Still Waters*

"*The Guy,* by Marilyn Wolf, delves into the intricacies of human emotions, relationships, and life experiences. With a unique blend of lyrical beauty and raw honesty, *The Guy* is a testament to Wolf's exceptional talent as a poet."
— Angela Jackson-Brown, author of *Untethered*

"Free verse is outside my comfort zone. Having said that—I was pulled in and hooked early on. I wanted to know how it ended. I couldn't put it down until I had read it all. The emotions are spot on. Raw, real, authentic. The drawings enhance the verse. I fully recommend it."
— Gloria J. Danielson, RN, JD

Also By MARILYN WOLF

In Celebration of the Death of Faeries

https://wolfen25.net

The Guy

by Marilyn Wolf

Table of Contents

Life was a maelstrom 1

creates a Life 3

alone again 4

weekly reports 5

mischievous smile 7

curiosity 7

schedule a meeting 7

tall and muscled 9

walking in a park 11

I want to kiss you 13

snuggles into his hands 15

Thank you for lunch 16

silent treatment 17

Short 19

it's casual to him 20

why now 21

I'll buy you dinner 23

buries his face 25

neighbor's BBQ 26

sound of his voice 27

casual conversation 29

in Her head 31

the call 33

naked in bed 35

Short 36

She misses him 37

massage 39

emotionally invested 40

hard won knowledge 41

ANGRY SEX!!! 43

mixed signals 45

introspection 47

"enough" 49

urgency in his hands 51

it's him 53

for any reason 55

another's home 56

despair and loneliness 57

booty calls 58

last first kiss 59

scented candles 61

only sharing his light 63

keeping all this up 65

seduction 67

Drama 68

Her Guy 69

one last visit 71

tattooed on Her Heart 72

he changed Her 73

eagle tattoo 75

Notes 76

Publication Acknowledgement: 77

five years
Life was a maelstrom
of emotional horror

death: husband   dogs   mom
broken heart [1]
depression
widow's brain [2]
lost track of time
hives   pimples   shingles
not eating for days
lost more than 75 pounds
multiple surgeries
scammed
moved five times in less than three years
suicidal plans

now
Tall and Her dog
start over in a new city
knowing one person

a new Life chapter

the story begins

creates a Life from scratch
We can do this, Pupper.

takes cookies to the neighbors
makes marshmallow people for the kids
talks to other dog walkers
plays cards at the Legion
shoots pool at the local tavern

meets an amazing group of women

We're off and running, Baby Girl!

alone again after decades
Tall sets up online dating
 several sites
 profiles
 men
until the men replying meet Her standards

online dating is not for the faint of heart
thousands of choices
hundreds of rejections
 received and given

fish pic   no
top of his head   no
ungroomed beard   no
bad teeth   no

wanting to be touched   yes
hearing a man's voice   yes
laughing   yes
breath on skin   yes

swipes left   swipes right

another first-date lunch
another man She'll never talk to again

weekly reports to Her women friends:
two Daves this week
Jim fell off
Tom turned out to be married
may spend the weekend in Michigan
they all laugh

She wades through this for a year
then sees The Guy's profile

finally: an exceptionally cute
sexy   tall   man
Tall loves the mischievous smile
when it says   *Well, hello, Darlin'*

deep tan   white hair   broad shoulders   big hands
already feeling his beard against Her skin
in Her bedroom
She bares Her neck
breathes deeply

Tall watches his profile for days
anticipating his pictures
Her mouth waters
   at the thought of a response

a dog with a bone:
She likes every photo of him
pursues him
messages him   eager for a reply
unbidden grin when a reply comes
Her heart rate   skin   temperature rise

The Guy has a dozen emails
who is this woman?
is She stalking me?
curiosity won't let him ignore Her
he signs on   reads Her posts
fun pictures   great breasts   great legs

sends a reply

they schedule a meeting in the off-
   screen world
      of sweat & muscle
      nerves & determination
Tall will take him as far as he'll let Her
She already knows   She'll eat him alive

7

his motorcycle roars and vibrates
pulling into the lot

tall and muscled
The Guy dismounts
Tall vibrates like the motorcycle

Her tank top shows
a tattoo
King of Hearts—
    big breasts big tattoo
he has tattoos
    asks to see it

She pulls Her shirt and bra
down to show most of it
The Guy touches Her breast
with one finger
pulls Her bra
& top down more
the nipple almost bare—
She doesn't stop him

Her breath quickens   pupils dilate
The Guy has big   gorgeous hands
smooth skin   flat nails   square fingers
—eager to touch & be touched by them

Did you notice how I didn't
have any problem touching you?

Did you notice how I didn't
have any problem letting you?

they order a pizza
half meat   half veggies

My half is real pizza.
Yours is cardboard and grass.

makes Her chuckle
he's a funny guy

he's wearing a zip hoodie
Tall thinks about
sliding Her hand under it
stroking his ribs and belly

they can't part after pizza
still touching   bodies tingling
walking in a park
The Guy laughs
puts Tall's arm around his waist
his around Hers
teenagers — tender   touching   tantalizing   tempted   tremulous
the joy at being together
expands into the sunshine
surrounds them

a bench the color of weathered mahogany
hangs by thick black chains
they swing   chat:
      hands   arms   thighs   hips   shoulders
      against
      hands   arms   thighs   hips   shoulders

breaths come quickly eager for more
neither says it but both know
he touches Her   Her heart leaps
She sees his pupils dilate

a man walks his little dogs past
      both dogs come over for petting
      he's surprised
      they don't usually like strangers

The Guy and Tall   both "dog people"
dogs know

She starts to hug him

full velvet lips touch Hers
pushes Her head onto his shoulder
lips and tongue move over Hers
She replies
soft   urgent   luscious kisses
four breasts tingle
four nipples at attention

after those kisses
She wants him in Her bed
strong silken hands to roam Her body
kiss Her skin
under over Her
four legs to entwine
slide against each other

they stand belly pressed to belly
Her arms around his neck

Tall feels him grow
neither want to leave

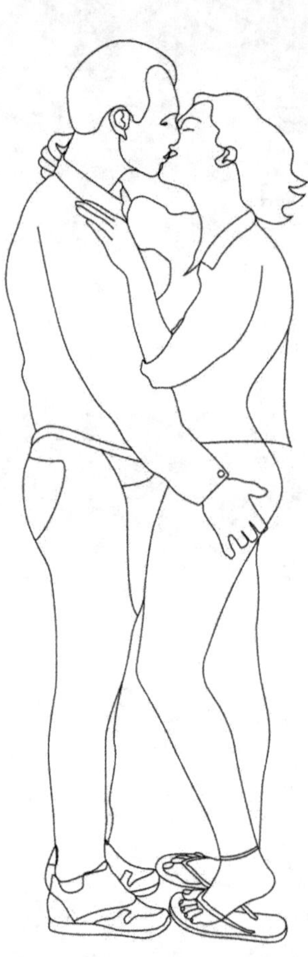

I've never dated anyone as tall as you.
You can almost look me in the eye.

naturally resting at ass high
Tall snuggles into his hands
  a perfect fit

they talk and kiss
    hug and stare
The Guy's eyes are the color
of the sky behind him

He thinks:
I wish She weren't wearing a sports bra
so I could tell how big those breasts really are
I HAVE to leave
Shit   I wish I hadn't
committed to dinner   maybe
I could get Her into bed

She wants those kisses
Come back to my place.

Blow them off. Come back with me.

Are you really, really sure?

I can't I have dinner plans.

I gotta leave.

I gotta leave.

this tall   handsome   sexy man
with desire in his eyes
and passion in his kisses

the ground can't catch Her
at how fast She's falling
for The Guy

he can't believe that butt
can't keep his hands or mind   off it
relishing it
his fingers react

I had a good time the other day.
Thank you for lunch. Tall says
    next day on the phone

                                        I had a good time too.
                            I kinda wish I had gone to your house
                                and stayed a little while longer,
                            but I might have gotten too handsy.

I was hoping you would.
Soon.

months later
She learns he didn't know
She really did want him to come back with Her

She would have taken him to bed that day
 fuck on a first date?
 Oh, Hell Yes!

The Guy thought She was just teasing

Some women mean yes *when saying* no.
My Yes *means* yes, *and* No *means* no.

Tall may flirt   pretend   tease   use innuendo
laugh at   Herself   him
She will not deceive or lie
play "games"
expect him act upon something She hasn't said
punish   use the silent treatment
withhold sex

Tall may be too in-your-face
but he won't have to guess where he stands
The Guy hasn't realized that yet

She finds out later
he never will

The Guy had broken off a relationship
six months before he met Tall

     right after
Short: a decades-long friend and widow
started spending weekends at his place
ostensibly
          to get away from her kids

sure
          as likely as a toad huggin' a fly

eventually they had sex
The Guy thought it just happened

silly man
Short engineered it
of course

                                                  he says
                                          it's casual to him
                        it's possible she'll get a boyfriend one day and
                              we'll have to stop doin' what we're doin'

                                          he's still looking at other women
                                          still checking the dating sites

but he's fucking two women: Tall and Short
he's lusty and conflicted
the women don't know about each other

emotionally and physically
    he   can't   keep   up

why now? he thinks
when I'm already fucking Short
why couldn't I have met Her first?

Tall has completely
taken over my thoughts.
I can't be around Her
without wanting to be in Her.

I wish She lived closer   so I could
ravage Her   whenever I want.
I think about Her   when I go to bed
              and   when I wake up
              and   while I'm at work.

I know where I'll be Saturday.

while in Her driveway
sitting on his motorcycle
She tells him
I'll buy you dinner sometime,
If you want to come out.

he's there the next Wednesday
he looks just as yummy
as the first time She saw him

Tall wants more of that
No   She wants ALL of that

ALL of him
under Her hands   &   legs   &   mouth
in Her bed

they have a wonderful time
 sitting across from each other
talking   eating   laughing
 he leaves to go to the restroom
 comes back
 scoots in tightly beside Her

he wants to feel Her
as much as She wants to feel him
touching from shoulder to ankle
they   laugh   talk

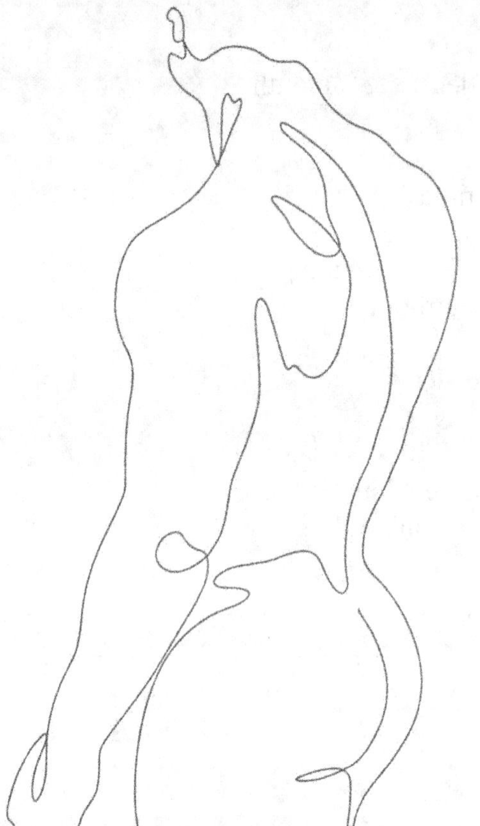

back at the house: playtime
he sits in a chair
pulls Her hips to him
lifts   shirt   bra
takes a nipple in his mouth
buries his face in Her breast
only the bridge of his nose showing

his arms hold Her tightly
their breaths quicken   skin flushes
his fingers dig into Her back
She arches into his face
     breath races out
though the window is open
their air is hot

hands on his shoulders
She pushes him back
takes his hand
leads him to bed

Her clothes fall off like butter on hot corn
he undresses to reveal
     slow rolling hills   gentle valleys
       of shoulders back butt legs
     miles and miles of skin like warm water

I can't have sex with you.

WTF?
Why did you get naked then?

I want Her RIGHT NOW!
This isn't right.
I'm already dating Short, he thinks

his body decides tonight's the night
gliding over Her thigh
slips into Her
She parts around him

pressure builds   forces moans from mouths

over too soon   he leaves soon after
to get up early for work

Tall gets off two more times thinking about him

Tall is invited to a neighbor's BBQ
on a weeknight
the neighborhood will be there
    adults   kids   dogs   one cat
She invites The Guy

before: playtime
mouth and hands on and in
tasting   feeling   smelling
hungry for each other
            more than BBQ

across the street
everyone has a good time
talking   laughing   eating
he helps himself to the food
along with everyone else
   BBQ   beans   salad   cherry pie
        bourbon   soda
they like him
She likes him

too soon   disappointed
they leave first
he must get up early for work

quick kiss at the door
he's gone

She sees everyone else around the fire pit

It's a little early for you to be using
Baby and Sweetie   he says

Whut?
You've called me Babe & Darlin'

lighten up
I call the clerk at the grocery Baby

they phone & text every day
he fills the room
through the phone

Tall likes hearing about his day
the sound of his voice makes Her smile

                                              the phrases he uses make Her smile:
                                he's done couples pattern dancing for decades
                                    unstructured dancing is *freeform ass shakin'*

sometimes they talk for two
hours or more   he wears
his headset   talking as he goes
through his evening
fixing dinner
working on his trailer
crunching peanut M&Ms®

She carries the phone
walking Her dog
fixing dinner
washing dishes
watching tv

friends first

sex without friendship
won't last

The Guy comes out
they have sex
he feels wonderful!

                                                  moans   *Oh My Lord*   a couple times

they get dressed
sit out back   talk
he smokes
       gentle breeze lifts the smoke
              away from them
dogs bark
pickup drives past
goldfinch lands on evergreen's
       very top branch
       bright yellow against dark green
breeze cools sex-soaked skin

casual conversation about anything   everything
builds comfort and trust

they waltz around each other
two step
learning   calculating
  the likelihood
    of smiles   and sex

I've been awake
for more than two
hours with my head
full of you, again

I would love to be able to
reach out
cup your ass
snuggle breasts belly against your back
cup your thigh with my knee
slide a foot down your calf
stroke your foot with mine
until the length of me
is against the length of you

Tall wants him
in Her bed
in Her head
in Her heart
in Her home
in Her future

She wants to
buy groceries
cook
go to the beach
have sex   on the beach
watch tv   dance in the kitchen
ride the motorcycle   enjoy the scenery
feel the vibration between Her legs
talk about the day

with him

She wants to share
joy & sadness
health & sickness

with him

make love
every day in every way

with him

She didn't expect to like him
so much so quickly
She's as surprised as he is

sex is already fantastic
She imagines how much
better they can get

(She mistakenly thinks they have a lot of time
to learn
how to make each other feel good
learn each other's preferences)

his birthday is a week from Monday
Tall invites him to dinner over the weekend
son & daughter-in-law   if he wants

he's   noncommittal
She doesn't understand
these past weeks have been positively joyous!

then
She gets

        the call

You're not gonna like what I have to say.
I'm dating someone else, too.
I'll be at her house this weekend.
You can't call or text until Sunday night.

shit

She sobs

now She knows
why She can't stay overnight

his neighbors might notice
or his son
      might show up unannounced

joy he shares with Tall
hobbled
by loyalty to Short

that explains short visits
hesitancy at   Babe   Darlin'
no overnights

        shit

naked in bed at Her place he asks
Why do you smile when you look at me?

I smile because I can't not smile
She must let him in
no defenses to keep him out
he fills the broken places
left by the deaths of husband   dogs   mom
he brings joy with
calls   texts   just walking in the door

he's already tattooed
    himself on the inside of Her skull

No one else feels that way about me.

how sad for you
that I may be the only one

Tall decides to go
to the dance hall
listen to the music
watch people dance
shoot some pool

biggest Midwest dance floor
country line dancing fame
couples pattern dancing
Jason Aldean concert
  thousands of people
 music & muscle
  bars   beers   bellies   butts
  boots   boobs   bands   bourbon
  pool cues & cuties
    flashing lights   dark corners
  dancing & drinking
singing   swaying   swinging
impossible to walk in a straight line

She glances up
The Guy is dancing
She doesn't know if he's alone
She doesn't tell him She's there

he enjoys it so
he's good at it
watching him makes Her happy

clearing the pool table makes Her happy too

from comments he makes
his social media
Tall learns who Short is
what she looks like

She doesn't tell him She knows

loyalty vs lust
dating two women brings heavy guilt
he can hardly manage

Tall is being shredded
under the spinning wheels
of his education

She doesn't hear from him for a while
Tall goes on about Her life
movies and dinners with girlfriends
an occasional fuck buddy
taking care of Her dog
cleaning out mom's house
tying up the estate
talking to the lawyer

Tall misses all of him
talking to him
        deep   warm   voice
the way he walks
        a dance athlete
watching him dance
        smooth flow
        quick changes
        memorized patterns
his body
   (both clothed and naked)
She misses him
with or without him Her Life doesn't stop

he's never had backrubs like Hers
or a complete massage

Your massages are amazing!

tense muscles soften under Her hands
he relaxes

*What do you want me to do
if you go to sleep?*

I won't go to sleep.

*What do you want me to do
if you go to sleep?*

I won't go to sleep.

three hours later he awakes
Tall is gone

Tall'd like to touch him in the night
listen to him breathe
   angry   jealous   sad
that Short's welcome in his bed at night
and She's not

The Guy feels guilty thinking about Tall
guilty when he wants Her
more guilty after he's had Her
loyal to Short
lust for Tall

She and girlfriends discuss:
*The Guy
the fuck buddies
The Youngster (younger than Her kids)
other men off the dating sites*
on Saturday mornings
over coffee

with The Guy at Her place
to fuck and talk
Tall is making love   he isn't
She is emotionally invested already
he is but doesn't want to be

Her on the bottom   full of him
his belly blooms
from narrow hips

his nipples hard
skin changing color

belly fills Her vision
belly   face   belly   face
as he fills Her throat again and again

I'm really good at sex
I didn't get good by wishing I could be
I went out & screwed around
            hard won knowledge
                though very useful

My husband knew and appreciated my talents
The Guy is just learning

ANGRY SEX!!! She shouts

What do you mean you don't know what that is?

When a woman's mad at me,
I know I won't get sex for days.
Maybe weeks.

How sad for you.
This is the punishment
I mentioned earlier.
Remember?

    angry sex is more
        a tornado   violent and twisted
    not just a storm
        fangs and claws
    not just teeth and nails

bite him
suck him
ride him
not hurt him
 too badly…

not making love
that's for sadness and intimacy

ANGRY SEX!!! is its own reward

The angry person gets to use
 not wear
 the handcuffs.

43

Tall is angry at The Guy
casual sex with Short makes him feel guilty
with any form of sex with Her
    even wanting Her makes him feel guilty
    loyalty vs lust

She's horny
She wants to make love
  taste his kisses
  touch his face
  feel him fill any part of Her

Her country chimera
is giving mixed signals
    joy & passion
when he wants to be there
    guilt & lust
because he can't stay away

Tall is not   ever   allowed to just show up
The Guy wants to keep Her a secret from everyone
especially Short
and neighbors

so   She takes matters in hand
several times

ANGRY at him
ANGRY at Short
swollen   panting   still horny

fuck you both

sitting out back   talking
    at Her place
  sunshine   eases confidences   introspection
    gazing into the past brings words to the present
      he mouths but doesn't feel
      as if reading a journal
    words of pain and sadness
      unbidden tears go unnoticed

*I blamed my ex for years then realized my role in the
breakup. I don't know if I can avoid making the same
mistakes. I tried for eight years with the next one. In the
end, I loaded up what I could carry and drove cross-
country. Six months on the next one. That one broke up,
too. I don't know how to have a successful relationship.
I'm scared to try again. I don't want to hurt another
woman or me.*

lost in himself
soft breeze carries a butterfly past
cigarette ashes fall off
  he doesn't notice
  She doesn't care
breeze lifts smoke   memories
  to follow the butterfly
  all disappear
his cigarette burns to the filter

his memories become a third person

Tall will do Her best to be patient
consistent
take cues from him
between them
someday maybe he'll trust Her
enough to see Her as his "safe place"
where he will choose to come
when the world is just too much

She will be patient until he's ready

*There are so many things
I'd like to do to and with you in bed.
So few opportunities to try them out…*

The Guy tells Tall:
Sex with her is casual.
I have amazing sex with you!
You have better equipment and more experience than her.
I can't be around you without intense sexual tension.
You and I will have sex again because I can't stay away forever.
I fantasize about you.
I look at your pictures probably more often than I should.
Your massages are amazing!
I never need a pill for sex with you.

Tall is statuesque   svelte   smart   strong   sexy   skilled
Short is so —   not

but nothing Tall does or says or is
will ever be "enough"
he won't let Her be enough
loyal to Short
lust brings him back to Tall

Everything happens when it's supposed to

does The Guy even consider:
maybe Tall happened now
because
it's time for him to stop doin' what he's doin' with Short?

The Guy keeps coming and going
guilt keeps him away
lust brings him back

they used to talk for hours every day
no topic was off limits

…now there are no topics
  at all
…because there is no talking
  at all

they have sex
the day they move the furniture to Her new home

everyone else left
he could have   chose not to
they sit outside & talk
She sees his pants begin to bloom

inside they try the usual
he can't come
something different solves the problem
using skills She learned the hard way

lust in his eyes
passion in his kisses
urgency in his hands
his guilt is heavy
he's never dated two women at the same time
loyalty vs lust
he wants Her
and they both know it

I didn't want to.
I can't believe you talked me into it.

She didn't have to talk too hard…
he gets dressed   leaves
it was the last time She saw him for weeks
    again

The Guy makes Tall CRAZY!
dating him is like living
an arm's length from
a railroad track
with an unknown train schedule
he thunders past
fills Her senses
rattles Her world
then disappears

Her day melts watching him drive away   again
        they are every country song on every radio

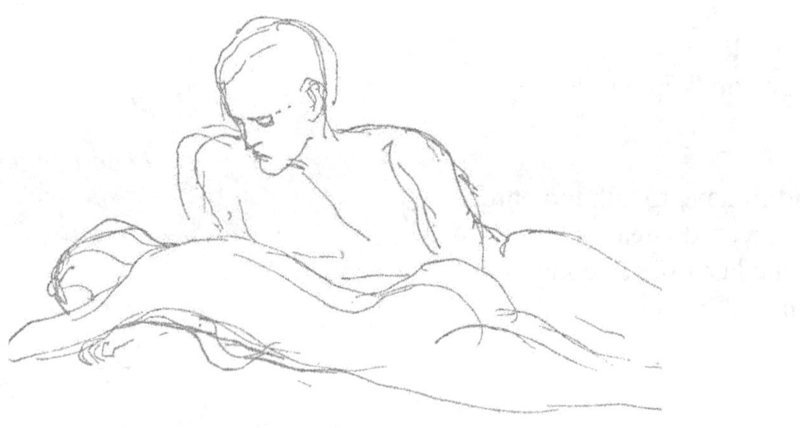

hanging out with Her dog
              14yo Molly
just back from their walk with dinner started
She watches TV

poor baby
they've moved so often
Molly gets nervous when
    Tall moves furniture to clean

the phone rings
it's him
after months
apparently
    they're talking again

he tells Her
he thinks of Her
          …with lust
      there's that word again

She feels him growing
through the phone

The Guy is welcome
in Her home and Her bed
at any time
for any reason
even if there's already someone else in it

he has a key
he can let himself in

  for any reason
  or no reason

The Guy is welcome in Her home and Her bed at any time for any reason

these are all reasons one friend might visit another's home:

to celebrate, share a bath or shower, sunbathe, swim, , tell a new joke, deliver flowers, accompany them on a trip, connect, feel connection, apologize or ask for forgiveness, seek or become a shoulder to cry on, quilting bee, raise a barn, panty raid, drop off gifts, get warm, Intellectual or creative stimulation, emotional support, intellectual reassurance, share joy or sadness, get a massage, hold hands, get to know them more intimately than meeting in public, share a home-cooked meal, share a hobby, meet their pets, receive honest feedback, break up, make up, brag, see their new pet, shovel snow, make it look like the owner is home, get the mail, solve a mystery, hide from someone, empty the fridge, borrow or return something, make new friends, wish them a Happy Holiday, do research for a book being written, interview someone, sort help with home care or Hospice care, make love, help a short friend with a task requiring height, you like me, offer a second pair of hands, see a hobby collection, hang out, get advice, play music together, spend time together, escape a nagging spouse/partner, your bed is cold and mine is already warm, watch a tv show, help with a project, have sex, bring over dip and chips to munch during the movies, hash out a problem, hide from the world for a bit, share a success or disappointment, meet their friends, make love, fix something, lend a hand, give an opinion, give a massage, help move something, chat, babysit, sit by a fire or bonfire, make love, create a fellowship for a quest, bake cookies, give a massage, check on the house, hang out, make love, cook together, eat together, get warm, let the dog out, see a friend

extend empathy or sympathy, babysit, make love, house sit, give someone a ride, companionship or visit, have a play date with kids or dogs, pet or play with their dog, let them play with your dog, share a hug, fix something, caregiving have a duet or play music, touch another in the night, listen to breathing in the dark, was invited, bring comfort, invite them to get a meal, ask a favor, run errands, watch a movie, share a meal, get a ride, was invited, family

She wishes he'd stay sometime

The Guy tells Her he cries from
despair and loneliness
She knows he wants to feel safe

Who gets to know all your sadness?
Who holds you when you cry?

She hopes he finds the person who will
to be the answer to those questions
She wants this for both of them
they each deserve that person
   even if it's not each other

when he feels down
he looks around and realizes
there's no shoulder for him to lean on

been alone since
he was 17   just a kid
to take care of himself
tears in his eyes
emotion bubbles
just below the surface
he won't set it free
he backs off
making sure She doesn't
get too close emotionally

Does he let anyone get close?

though Tall knows
The Guy is lonely
he fervently resists letting Tall or Short
get close to him
straight arm to the face: *Stay away from me!*

he would rather stay alone with
his specters of fear and loneliness
than be with either Tall or Short

The Guy   Fear   Loneliness
   became a triad

from Tall's perspective
Fear and Loneliness are holding
the cards in this game

The Guy thinks he hasn't heard from Her because
She's "busy" with booty calls
nope

Unlike you,
I'll talk to whomever I want
whenever I want.
If the person I'm with doesn't like it
they can move along.

I won't deliberately
make anyone uncomfortable
but neither will I blow off one friend
 for another

Like you do to me.

She hoped
Her last first kiss
would be The Guy
he isn't interested
kissing another is bittersweet

Tall and Molly take a nap in the evening
She strokes shiny fur as they fall asleep
when they wake up
their usual love fest
    of cuddles and stroking

She wants to stroke The Guy   too

The Guy invites Tall over
spice-scented candles burn
they shower   make love   play
          smile   laugh   talk
they haven't played for too long

She told him months ago
She loves him
not telling felt dishonest
if he does love Her
 loyalty won't let him admit it

Short came down last weekend
The Guy told Tall not to call or text
while Short was there   as usual

he has known Short for decades
through spouses   kids   jobs

Short will always have priority on his time
because he feels guilty about seeing Tall
he will make Tall cry but never Short
Short still doesn't know about Tall

The Guy and Tall start talking again
after months without
he wanted to see Her
guilt kept him away
lust brought him back

he misses Her body & how She makes him feel
She doesn't know if he missed Her as a person
She doesn't ask
She only asks questions
when ready to hear the answers

if the answer is no She's not ready to hear it

he is only sharing his light with Her
playful shafts touching nothing
touching everything
hiding   following   preceding
wrapping   dancing
She can play with it
        be in it
but hold none of it

he will never give Her the lamp

Tall's still dating others
they come; they go

keeping all this up gets so tiring
today She can feel Loneliness around Her edges
the worst part is
remembering suicide
    is a viable escape

She works through the Sadness now
still working on welcoming Loneliness   though
seriously misses being part of a couple

The Guy will only commit to Short
he won't make Short cry
Short still doesn't know about Her

Tall plans a full-on seduction for The Guy

building anticipation of the event She sends
 notes   pictures   texts

black   lacy lingerie
    easily removable layers
low lighting   candles
       blues playing softly
The Guy nude or loose shorts
          (so She can watch him react)
Tall in front of him   straddling   a lone wooden chair
dance   strip tease   make it last
touch him   he cannot return the touch
doing whatever he wants or what She can
          pull from Her bag of tricks
finally let him touch Her

aftercare: full body massage
gentle stroking   sleep

share the same bed
stretch out along
the length of him
wake up together

it never happens…

he goes to see
Short that weekend

Drama

a year ago today
the last time
Tall made love to The Guy

if he was making love to Her
loyalty wouldn't let him admit it
damn him!

they both enjoyed it
 too much — She didn't hear
from him for months   again
loyalty vs lust   again

in between
She met a partner: Her Guy
    fell in love

They each have
new lives
    Tall with Her Guy
    The Guy with Short

only the friendship remains

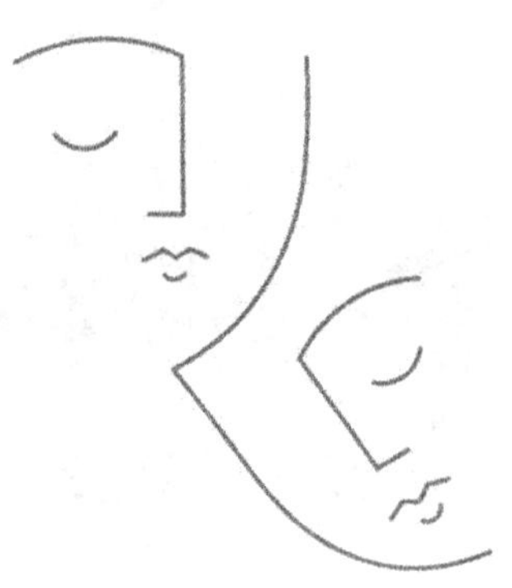

one last visit
most likely   their last goodbye
before they go
their separate ways

when they see each other
  joy expands
    and surrounds them

big hugs
big smiles

not like when they first met:
the joy of possibilities

this is a joy of:
shared memories   familiarity

finality
fills the room
both feel its fingers
gripping   pulling apart

parting brings tears to both

whether he wants to be or not
The Guy is
tattooed on Her Heart

the Universe sent him
when She desperately needed him

The Guy rose from the ashes of Her last five years

he doesn't understand what a difference
he made in Her life
he brought
joy   laughter   fun

Tall hasn't sought
fun in YEARS
She is now

he changed Her

because of him
She wants a life
She's able to make a life
instead of being buffeted by whatever comes along…

he saved Her life

Her new eagle tattoo symbolizes
    freedom
        from sadness and darkness
    strength
        to choose a path
        that builds not destroys
        mental health
    resilience
        to keep going
        when it doesn't seem possible
    courage
        to make those choices

Tall and Her eagle

are taking on the world!

Cover   *Standing Male Figure*, John Singer Sargent (1856-1925), commons.wikimedia.org

1   [1] Schafer, J. (2016, December 29). Broken Heart Syndrome, Two hearts, one beat. *Psychology Today*. https://www.psychologytoday.com/us/blog/let-their-words-do-the-talking/201612/broken-heart-syndrome

1   [2] Stanford, C. (2014, October 16). Understanding Widow Fog. *The Widows Foundation*. https://thewidowsfoundation.nl/welcome-welkom-bienvenue/english/medical-information/brain-health-menu/widow-brainwidow-fog/understanding-widow-fog-part-i/

2   Ken Reid. Phantom 2. Unsplash.com. June 20, 2017.

6   IrinaSol. ID: 2291545363. Shutterstock.com (licensed by author)

8   Eroshka. ID: 1862937193. Shutterstock.com (licensed by author). Card scanned by author.

10   DODOMO. ID: 1554298949. Shutterstock.com (licensed by author).

12   moopsi. ID: 1248714790. Shutterstock.com (licensed by author).

14   Fiverr.com. Image licensed by author.

18   Krag, Eiler. *An ABZ of Love,* p. 221. Medical Press of New York. 1963.

22   Simple Line. ID: 1993885886. Shutterstock.com (licensed by author).

24   ID: 2014080815. Shutterstock.com (licensed by author).

28   ID: 1798196. clipart-library.com

30   Schiele, Egon. *Squatting Girl*. commons.wikimedia.org

32   Barnawi M Thahir. ID: 2206490871. Shutterstock.com (licensed by author).

34   Krag, Eiler. *An ABZ of Love,* p. 49. Medical Press of New York. 1963.

38   Krag, Eiler. *An ABZ of Love,* p. 232. Medical Press of New York. 1963.

42   Krag, Eiler. *An ABZ of Love,* p. 249. Medical Press of New York. 1963.

44   Schiele, Egon. *Reclining Girl.* commons.wikimedia.org

46   Askhat Gilyakhov. ID: 1415411801. Shutterstock.com (licensed by author).

48   Used with artist's permission. Licensed by author.

50   Krag, Eiler. *An ABZ of Love,* p. 277. Medical Press of New York. 1963.

52   Krag, Eiler. *An ABZ of Love,* p. 156. Medical Press of New York. 1963.

54   Schiele, Egon. *Propping up Female Nude with Long Hair.* commons.wikimedia.org

60   Krag, Eiler. *An ABZ of Love,* p. 150. Medical Press of New York. 1963.

64   Krag, Eiler. *An ABZ of Love,* p. 270. Medical Press of New York. 1963.

66   Krag, Eiler. *An ABZ of Love,* p. 33. Medical Press of New York. 1963.

70   Dan Thoner. ID: 1362424811. Shutterstock.com (licensed by author).

74   Mari Muzz. ID: 2060217221. Shutterstock.com (licensed by author).

Publication Acknowledgement:
The only poem previously published is:
  Wolf, M. "She Will Never Own the Lamp." Medium.com/Move Me Poetry. 2023.
  https://medium.com/move-me-poetry/she-will-never-own-the-lamp-49cf8b46dad4

Thank you to my friends, colleagues, and fellow authors who read, and
re-read, many versions of *The Guy*. You helped enormously with finding
clunky wording, misspellings, and more while giving me your suggestions
gently and consistently. I very much appreciate and am grateful for your
time, knowledge, and expertise.

    Arianna Grazzani
    B. K. Ray
    Bob Webster
    David Allen
    Jack Mitenbuler
    John Hinton
    Mike Nierste
    Maureen Brustkern
    Thomas Kneeland